Santa's Pleasure

Books by Porsha Deun

<u>The Love Lost Series</u>
Love Lost
Love Lost Forever
Love Lost Revenge

<u>The Addict Series</u>
Addict—A Fatal Attraction Story
Addict 2.0—Andre's Story
Addict 3.0—DeAngelo's Story
Addict 4.0—DeMario's Story

<u>The Hot Holiday Series</u>
Santa's Pleasure
Cupid's Lust (Coming February 2025)
Jacks Thrills (Coming October 2025)

<u>Standalones</u>
Intoxic
In Over Her Head

<u>Children's Book</u>
Princesses Can Do Anything!

SANTA'S PLEASURE. Copyright © 2024 by Porsha Deun. All rights reserved. Printed in the United States of America for Porsha Deun, LLC. For information, email Porsha Deun, porshadeun@gmail.com.

All characters, places, and events are fiction and not real. Any likeness is a coincidence and not intentional.

All rights reserved. No parts of this book may be reproduced by any mechanical, photographic, or electronic process, or in the form of a phonographic recording; nor may it be stored in a retrieval system, transmitted, or otherwise copied for public or private use—other than for "fair use" as brief quotations embodied in articles and reviews—without prior written permission of the author.

ISBN (paperback): 979-8-9901518-2-6

ISBN (eBook): 979-8-9901518-3-3

To the Black plus-size girlies

who just wants to get some and move on.

Get it, Queen.

Santa's Pleasure

The Saturday After Thanksgiving

I sigh. "Why am I even here?"

"Because you promised me you'd not only show up but also stay for at least an hour," my cousin says with a smile that tells me she is growing impatient with my impatience.

"I'm making a mental note to never do that again." We continue to walk around the crowded hall owned by a local biker's organization, checking out the vendor tents. Well, at least Tamia is checking them out. I'm looking at the tacky painting on the cinderblock walls and grungy windows that are too high and too small for anyone to get through if they need to escape a fire or a crowded holiday vendor event. I realize I'm the only person the latter applies to.

"Crissy, do some shopping."

"You know I could have stayed home and shopped from my phone, right?"

"That's not supporting local artisans and businesses," Tamia quips. "Plus, you need to get out of the house sometimes. I know you love your books and don't like crowds, but you need to interact with people, too."

"There are people in my books and crowds of those on my bookshelves."

"Real. People," say says through gritted teeth.

"Are there any local authors in here?"

"That's not—"

"Local authors qualify as both artisans and businesses."

Now she sights, frustrated to have lost this battle. "Fine! Go, just don't leave! Meet me here in an hour."

"Yes, mom," I say mockingly, and she shakes her head at me. Tamia is by far my favorite relative. Our twin mothers raised us together like sisters, even dressing us the same when we were kids. However, Tamia is definitely the most outgoing one among us, much like my mother. While I'm more reserved, like her mother. We always joke that an angel switched our personalities while the twins, our moms, were pregnant.

Santa's Pleasure

I walk around the event hoping to find a table with an indie author or indie bookstore. Every room in my house, except the bathroom, has at least a floating bookshelf, but most have a series of them and a wall of bookcases. Books work as both pleasure and décor.

As I continue pass the tables of jewelry, clothing, gift baskets, I come across one with journals and adult coloring books with Black women on the covers. *A book girlie can never have too many journals.* I pick out three journals, five coloring books, some bookmarks, and a couple of pens with affirmations on them. While the seller is packaging my items, I notice the vendor at the next table… noticing me.

Smooth midnight skin.

Male.

Full beard.

Full lips.

Definitely taller than six feet.

Built like The Rock and wearing a fitted red turtleneck, jeans, and a Santa hat.

When my eyes return to his after roaming over his body, he's biting his lip, and I do the same. He knows he has my attention.

Mr. Sexy chuckles at something before nodding to his side and looking from me to the merchant I'm purchasing from, then back to me.

Looking at her, she's holding my bag out to me. By the look on her face, she must have been trying to get my attention, and I didn't hear her.

"Sorry," I mumble.

She gives me a tight smile and then a warning. "You want nothing to do with him. He's offering his *pleasure services.*"

"Pleasure services?" I whisper back.

"Yeah. You know, *pleasure,*" she says while looking me up and down. "He's here every year selling himself to women. He even has the nerve to hourly and nightly rates. I could never be that desperate."

"Hmph." Little does this woman know, she did nothing but give me every reason to go to his table. *No strings attached sex?* She has no idea how perfect that sounds to me.

With the most seductive walk I can muster in my navy peacoat and tall black stiletto boots, I saunter over to his table. "So, I hear you are selling sex."

"Beautiful, and cuts right to the chase."

And he has an incredibly deep voice!

"Outside of family and a particular set of needs, I have little use for humans and small talk."

He stays quiet as I look over his pricing that includes everything from one-hour love sessions to a…

"What's included in the book boyfriend package?"

"Are you a romance reader?"

"I like my books Black, dark, with a touch of sweet."

"Mmmm. The book boyfriend package is an 18-hour package at a hotel, room fees not included in the cost. Most hotels check-in is at three and my client and I will belong exclusively to each other until check-out the next day. The add-on packages for additional time are not allowed, and we don't leave the room unless it is an emergency, or we need more ice. I will bring a bag of toys, oils, a massage table, and, of course, condoms.

"Prior to the arranged date, we will both submit to testing and share our result. We will discuss your preferred pet names, what you would feel comfortable calling me, soft and hard limits, and safe words. If you want, you can even pick out a scene or two from your favorite books for us to act out, or a theme."

"Theme? If I want you to treat me like you kidnapped me…"

"You would play the role of my victim with Stockholm syndrome turned lover."

I bite my lip again. "Ring me up for that."

"What's your name?" he asks as he picks up his tablet.

"Crissanya Harnett."

"Idris Odom." He passes me the tablet. "Put your information in."

"The dick better be damn good for these prices."

"You won't be complaining, trust me," he says with a cocky grin.

After paying, I continue around the venue, pretending to look at the tables. My mind's eye is full of visions of what is to come. I'm booking the hotel and scheduling my testing as soon as I get in my car. I buy a couple of books before heading back to the rendezvous point with Tamia.

"Did you buy anything other than books?"

"You'd be surprised. Thanks for dragging me out."

She gives me a curious look. "What the hell did you buy in there?"

Santa's Pleasure

I know I can tell Tamia anything and a part of me wants to tell her. But I decide this is something that's just for me. No one else will get to share in it, even vicariously.

Porsha Deun

The Day After Christmas

A month later, I'm riding up the hotel elevator with an overnight bag hanging off my shoulder. According to his text, Idris is already in the room. I wonder how he is going to pull off the kidnapping part of my fantasy. We discussed everything, just like he said we would. I decided I didn't want to do a particular book scene or a character from a book, but someone who's mentioned in stories I've heard since I was a child.

The doors slide open when the elevator arrives to the floor and Idris is standing there with no shirt on and the hat he wore when we met at the pop-up shop.

He smirks. "Don't scream."

Then he pounces, throwing a sack I didn't see over my head and then he throws me over his shoulder. *First the fuck of all... he just picked my deliciously plump ass up like it was nothing! Lawd, please don't let this dick be wack. I've paid too much money.*

He bends down and I hope he's picking up my dropped bag.

"Where are you taking me?" I say, getting into my role.

"Santa's workshop." Idris continues walking with me bouncing on his shoulder. I can't help but wonder what this may look like to anyone watching the hotel security camera feed. He stops and there is a beep. Not being able to see, I'm more aware of the sound of the door opening then closing, and Idris's footsteps. He throws me down harshly on the bed and I scoot backwards until I feel the pillows. For a few moments, I can hear him moving around the room, but then there is nothing.

"Who are you?"

"You don't recognize me as the man you used to set chocolate chip cookies out for as a child?"

"Since when has Santa been in the kidnapping business? Aren't you supposed to be giving out gifts?"

"I did that yesterday, but I thought it was time I get something for myself."

Santa's Pleasure

"So, you kidnapped me to be your next Mrs. Claus?"

He's moving again. The sack is yanked off my head and Idris, no, Santa, sits on the bed in front of me with a tray of fruit. "I kidnapped you to be my next ho, ho, ho."

"Whatever you think I'm about—"

"I don't think. I know." He picks up a grape from the tray and brings it to my lips. "Eat."

Pushing his hand away, I say, "I can feed myself."

He holds the grape in front of my lips again, but I silently refuse it. Santa nods and pops the grape into his mouth before standing and taking the fruit tray to the table on the other side of the room. "Suite yourself. Just know that is the last time you are going to refuse me."

"You can't make me do anything."

"I won't have to. We will both eat of our free will." Santa gives me a wicked grin. "You will give me your cookie."

I squeeze my legs together and it makes me feel my dampness all the more. So far, he is playing this up wonderfully. I'm so turned on right now.

He eats a few more grapes and some strawberries while never taking his eyes off me. "Take your coat off."

I don't.

He returns to the bed, but instead of sitting down, he stands next to me and stares me down. I stubbornly raise my chin. "We can both play that game, but I promise you, I will win," he says before bending down and scooping me up. I act like I fight against him while in my head I'm cheering. Santa sits on the bed and maneuvers me until I'm belly down and ass up over his lap with my arms restrained behind my back with his hands. He pushes the back of my coat up so he can see my ass that my dress barely covers in this position.

A single, loud thunderclap ricochets through the air and leaves my ass stinging. He repeats this until I scream. Lifting me from his lap, he lays me on my side.

"Take off your coat."

I do as I'm told, putting the coat on the bed next to me. Santa takes it and hangs it in the closet. When he returns to the main part of the room, he goes to the spread on the table and gathers some ice from the ice bucket.

"Lay on your stomach."

"I don't—"

"I'm soothing your ass with some ice. That's all."

Santa's Pleasure

I nod and turn over. He kneels beside me on the bed and lifts my dress up. The initial feel of the ice on my bare ass sends a shockwave through my body and I jump. "Easy, my sweet." I relax as he drags the ice across my skin, back and forth and around the straps of my thong. Low hums leave his mouth as he takes his time teasing me.

"You have the most beautiful ass."

"Thank you, Santa."

He moves the ice low on my ass, right where my thigh and ass meet. "May, I?"

"Yes, Santa."

He pushes the little left of the ice between my thighs and it melts in my juices, but Santa's fingers are still cold as they push further to explore more. "My sweet little whore is so fucking wet, and I'm suddenly famished. On your fucking knees."

I quickly raise up onto my knees, excitement and lust coursing through my veins. Keeping my chest as flat on the bed as my large breasts will let me, I make sure I'm perfectly arched for Santa. He gets off the bed and I hear him digging through a bag.

When he returns, something hard and cold like metal slides under my thong. "You won't be needing this."

Two slices on either side of the G-string and he pulls the thong off. He tosses it and it lands near my head.

He really cut my thong off. Before I can break character and say anything to him about it, the knife or scissors are cutting through my dress. "Whoa!"

"I'll get you another one or you can bill me."

He continues cutting up the back of my dress, through the shoulder straps, and he even cuts my bra straps. Santa spreads his hands across my back, pushing the remnants of my clothing off the sides of my body.

Whatever he used to cut my clothing with lands on the nightstand with a clank. In the next moment, Santa buries his face in my ass and licks me from clit to the top of my crack.

"Aaahhh."

He licks, sucks, nibbles, and dances his tongue from one end to the other. I told him I never had my ass ate and wanted to know what that feels like. Santa is showing me the experience is just as glorious as it is in the books I read.

Just when I think he's had his fill for now, he tells me to move further up the bed. I do and he lies on his back under me. "Sit down."

Santa's Pleasure

"What?"

"Sit. Down."

"Idris," I say, breaking character again, "I'm not trying to go to jail because you couldn't breathe."

"Thank you for your concern, but I'll be fine. Now, ass down on my face."

I lower myself down some and wait for him to commence.

"If you can't feel my face here," he lifts his head and licks my clit, "you aren't down far enough."

Spreading my knees further apart, I bring my ass closer to him. Santa wraps his arms round my thighs and brings me down even lower before he devours me again. He suckles on me like I'm fine dining. Soon, my worries about him breathing leave my head and I'm rotating my hips in small circles as he eats me.

I grab my titties to pinch and roll my nipples in-between my fingers as Santa eats me like it's his last supper. My body stiffens as a get close to orgasm and then I shatter. Quakes rip through me and my legs try to close around Santa's head, but he holds them open and doesn't let up on me.

"Santa! Santa! Shit, Santa!"

I have to put my hands on the headboard and wall in front of me to brace myself. My body shakes, rocks, and rolls through the orgasm as Santa expertly prolongs it with his tongue and lips. Based on the head game alone, I'm going to be a repeat customer of his.

Santa loosens his grip around my thighs, and I turn over, falling next to him on the bed in a dizzy pant. He turns on his side and captures my chin between his thumb and index finger, turning my head to force me to look at him. My eyes blink rapidly as my soul returns to my body.

"Are you ready to be Santa's little slut?"

I nod.

"Say it," he growls, and it sends a shiver down my spine.

"I'm ready to be Santa's little slut."

He brings his face so close to mine that I can taste my juices on his breath. "Good slut." He watches me as I react by biting my lip and smiling. Santa pulls away and adjusts his hat before walking over to a bag on the dresser. "Get in the center of the bed," he commands with his back towards me.

Santa's Pleasure

I watch him in the mirror in front of him as he looks for... I don't know what, as I shift to the center of the bed with my back against the headboard. His body rivals that of any sculpture of any gods of any nation. I've never seen a man with skin so dark and smooth that it looks like if you were to lick him, he would taste like your favorite chocolate bar. *I want to lick him... just one bicep to see.* When he finds what he's looking for, his dark brown eyes find mine in the mirror.

"Do you like what you see?"

"Very much."

He smirks and shakes a rolled black pouch at me. "Can you be still, or do you need to be restrained?"

"For what?"

Santa shakes his head.

"Restrain me." I hope this is the kink we discussed.

His hand dives into the bag again and comes up with a pair of leather cuffs. My breath quickens at the sight of them and I'm curious to know what's inside the cloth black roll. When he turns back to the bed, I get my first glimpse of his imprint and Santa appears to have that hammer, all capital letters and bold font. His undone jeans make it quite noticeable that he manscapes down there.

Fuck yes.

Santa chuckles and the baritone sound makes my already peaked nipples peak a little more. "See something else you like?"

"Yes, Santa. Can I taste it?"

"Soon enough."

I pout.

"Aht. You said you were going to be a good slut, remember?"

Switching from pouty to innocent facial expressions, I watch him as he sets the bulky wrap and cuffs on the bed.

"Lay down with your fingertips, just touching the headboard." When I do, he gives me a growl of approval.

"Has Santa ever considered doing voice acting for audiobooks?"

Santa smiles. "I've not, but you, my little slut, are not the first to tell me that."

I swear my pussy gets wetter every time he calls me that. "Your little slut thinks you should consider it. I myself would love to hear you voice over the works of my favorite authors in the near future."

Santa's Pleasure

"Maybe next time, Santa can read your favorite books to you while you bathe."

I don't know if he is looking forward to a next time or if he is just being a smart marketer and businessman, but it is working. "Maybe," I respond.

Santa gets onto the bed and straddles my body just below my breasts. He leans forward, reaching for my wrists. He smells of cocoa butter and musk and I can't help myself. Sticking my tongue out and slightly lifting my head, I lick around his navel. The chesty moan he gives urges me on. I lick and nibble at his taunt skin as he cuffs my wrists. My boobs block me from moving lower and getting to that smooth skin just above his dick. *Why does he still have these damn jeans on?*

"Your dick."

"What about it?"

"I want it between my breasts and in my mouth."

"Do you?"

"I do."

"Hmm. Pull your arms forward."

As he commanded, I pull my arms forward but am stopped. He's hooked the cuffs to something to keep my hands above my head. Having an hour of setup time before I arrived, Santa must have put something under the headboard or mattress just for this.

"Perfect," he says. "As for your request, you'll get that if you are a good slut for through this for me. Understand?"

"Yes, Daddy. I mean, Santa."

He bites his bottom lip. "Santa Daddy is good."

In my head, I remix the song. *Santa Daddy, please stick your dick between my titties… for me. I'll be a really good girl, Santa Daddy. So, stick your dick between my titties right now.*

He shifts down my body and takes a nipple into his mouth, making me hum the last note of the song. "Your titties are perfect," he says as he pushes them together, then sucks on my nipples simultaneously.

I pull against my restraints and wrap my legs around his body, desperate for the friction of his imprint against my clit. He matches my hip rotation while continuing sucking on my titties, and it isn't long before I'm cumming again.

"You know, that wasn't what I was about to do, but I couldn't resist these beautiful breasts," he says.

"Oh yeah. What were you about to do?"

Santa's Pleasure

Santa unrolls the black cloth, displaying a row of knives neatly contained in little sleeves. "They've been properly dulled, just as we discussed." He removes one and slides it over his skin to demonstrate. I appreciate him taking the time to build some trust between us as play partners.

"To make sure you remember, what are your safe words again?"

"Snow to slow down or ease up. Rudolph for full stop."

"Good job." He digs into his jeans pocket and pulls out a blindfold. Santa places it over my head. "Remember, if you are a good little slut, Santa will reward you with what you asked for."

"Yes, Santa Daddy."

"Mmmm. I really like the sound of that off your lips."

Again, my breath quickens from the anticipation of feeling the blade across my skin. I've read knife play stories, mostly in online fanfiction, that left me curious about how one gets pleasure from this kink. Impact play, I get and have done before. But knife play is a whole new world for me.

I first feel the blade inside my elbow, and I jump.

"Easy," Santa whispers.

The softness of his tone calms me as he drags the blade down the inside of my arm and over my breast. Santa is very gentle around my nipples as the knife teases along the sides of the hard buds. I moan softly as the knife continues down my torso. Then it is gone and I don't hear Santa. I pointlessly pull against the cuffs as if I can get up and search for him.

Fingers caress my cheek, easing my panic. He turns my face to the side, away from him, and the blade pulls along the thin skin of my neck and down my body. As the knife continues to send sensations all across and through my body, I understand how some can get off on sensory play. I'm grateful Santa blindfolded me, depriving me of one sensation to increase the awareness of another.

When he's done, I feel him lift off the bed and there is ruffling. I think he's removing his jeans. It isn't long before the thought is confirmed. Santa returns to the bed and straddles me just as he did before, and I can feel his dick laying between my breasts. Again, he leans forward, unshackling me from the leather cuffs, and the tip of his dick lands on my lips.

Santa's Pleasure

What is a girl supposed to do besides giving it a lick and suckle? I give it a little more than that as Santa's hips push forward to give me a little more. Soon he lifts over my breasts to give him better access to fuck my mouth. Once my hands are free, I remove the blindfold. Though his dick hasn't left my mouth since entering it, from what I can see of the base, the hammer is just as thick as the imprint of it appeared.

Santa works his hips back and forth, going deeper into my mouth with each stroke until he reaches the back of my throat, while I suck hard and work my tongue over the rigid skin of his dick. He thrusts forward and pushes into my throat.

"Good little slut! Fuck."

He gives my mouth long strokes, pausing every time he sinks all the way in. Each time he does, moans escape his mouth, and it is like candy to me. I like a vocal man.

Without warning, he pulls out and returns to his starting position. "Squeeze those titties together."

I do, enclosing his thick dick between them. Santa strokes his dick between my breasts, giving me everything I asked for. The sight of the head of his dick appearing and disappearing between my titties is everything I thought it would be. It turns me on so much that I want him to cum on them... now.

"Nut on my titties, Santa Daddy. Please, please, cover them with your cum," I beg.

"Oh, fuck." He strokes faster. "That's what you want?"

"Yes. Please, Santa Daddy."

A few more strokes and Santa gives me exactly what I want while he moans about what a good slut I am for him. He strokes his dick while releasing his nut on me. I massage his cum into my breasts while he watches and catches his breath. Santa leans down and puts a hand around my throat. "Is Santa's slut please?"

I bite my lip and nod.

"So is Santa. Now, go shower." He rises off of me and sits on the bed to give me room to get up. "Your bag is by the closet door."

While in the shower, I think about our time together so far. I don't know how long I've been in the room, but I've gotten off twice and him once. Yet, the dick hasn't touched the pussy. Just thinking about that long, thick dick with a hook to the side has me touching myself like I don't have whatever is left of the day and the rest of the night to feel him inside of me.

"Look at you," Santa says when he comes into the bathroom a few minutes later. I don't stop as he watches me through the glass door, stepping closer and closer with hunger in his eyes. "I thought you said you were pleased with your gift."

Angling my body, I give him a better view of me dj-ing my clit while I squeeze a titty with my other hand. "You gave me what I asked for." I say with a husky voice I don't recognize.

"But?"

"But I want more."

He smirks. "Is that how you ask?"

A quiver goes through my body. "Fuck me, Santa Daddy."

"Pretty…"

"… please."

This just made me think of the sexiest scene ever in a comic-book movie, despite the male love interest trying to kill the woman who went crazy loving him.

Santa steps into the walk-in shower and places two gold and black foil wrappers on the built-in shelf before giving me another hand necklace. "Good and greedy little slut."

He raises his other hand, which I didn't notice was holding a vine of grapes. Santa holds them above my head, and I take two of the bottom grapes into my mouth. After pulling the vine away, his mouth is immediately on mine. The mix of the steam in the shower, the juice and flesh of the grapes, the taste of my essence on his full lips, and my already turned on state are a head mix.

While kissing me, Santa's hand moves around to the side, then the back of my neck, massaging his fingertips into the base of my scalp under my shower bonnet. We both moan into the kiss as we feast on each other and more grapes.

Directing me by my head, Santa turns me around. "How mad would you be if I take this bonnet off?"

"Do you want to get back to the North Pole?"

He chuckles. "Understood."

Keeping his hand on top of my bonnet, he pulls my head back. I watch him from this position as he takes more grapes into his mouth, chews them, then bends down to feed them to me from his mouth. Santa releases my head, and the remaining grapes drop to the shower floor. I hear

Santa's Pleasure

the familiar sound of the gold foil wrapper opening behind me and my heartbeat picks up a little more in anticipation.

Moments later, Santa pulls back on my hips, and I brace my hands on the shower wall, awaiting his welcome intrusion. I release a long moan and close my eyes as he slides into my sweet spot.

"Damn, your shit is tight and warm as fuck."

I smile. "Just for Santa's pleasure."

"Mmmm."

He gives me full, long strokes and rocks his hips up and forward at the top to push deeper. My nails try and fail at digging into the vertically lined rectangular blue and gray tiles. I move my hips to match his tantalizing slow and steady rhythm.

"Pretty thick ass slut got some good pussy on you."

"Santa Daddy got some good dick on him," I moan back.

We continue in a melody of moans, grunts, ass slaps, and skin-on-skin claps with the shower as the background music until we both erupt in crescendo, our panting breaths serving as the breakdown at the end of a 90s R&B song.

After drying off in the shower, we order room service. At the table, in plush robes, we eat in silence, stealing glances at each other until he breaks the silence.

"Why are you single?"

"Because I choose to be."

"Why are you choosing that for yourself?"

"Outside of family, I don't like dealing with people and people don't know how to deal with me. Aspergers. I like sex, though, and it is better with a partner than by yourself. Outside of sex, the only people I prefer are fictional."

Santa nods as if he is taking my words in. "I wouldn't have thought you had Asperger's he day we met. You seemed so confident."

"I am with what I know I want. Outside of that, I dislike social gatherings. Even my being there was only because I promised my cousin I'd let her get me out of my house. She still insists on me 'touching grass'," I say with air quotes, "every now and then."

Not being able to help it, I roll my eyes, and he laughs.

"Typically, I also don't like people touching me unless we have agreed on the terms of engagement beforehand. That's why you and your business appeals to me. We discussed everything except the titty fucking, which I didn't realize I wanted until that moment. I don't need sex often, but when I do, I need to be thoroughly worn out. Then I'm good for months. Men, don't understand that, so it makes it hard for me to keep a steady sex partner."

"Spontaneity is hard for you."

Though he doesn't say it like a question, I nod. We sit in silence for a bit while picking over our food.

"I was serious about what I said earlier. You should really do voice acting for audiobooks. Indie authors are always looking for males with sexy voices to read and record their books. You could even have social media accounts where you take requests for short readings. With that growl of yours, the book girlies would go crazy over you."

"Another business venture doesn't sound bad." He studies me for a bit before continuing. "I'm thinking of taking on someone for this business."

"Another male sex worker?"

"Umm… yeah. Two actually. They look different from me, but most women would consider them handsome. One is Samoan."

I stare at him while imagining a Samoan man with a topknot and lush body holding me up on his shoulders while eating my papaya.

"Are you lusting over my potential business partners while sitting in front of me?"

"What?"

"You were biting your lip."

"Oh. Sorry."

"Do you think that would be a good idea?"

I shrug. "I don't know them. But it could expand the appeal of your business, bring in more women. You'd be able to take breaks between servicing women without having to lose money. Some women are going to want a threesome… or foursome."

Santa nods.

"Why did you tell me this?"

"You feel safe."

"I don't know what that means."

He opens his mouth and closes it again. "I'd know how to explain it."

"Now that, I understand."

We give each other smiles.

"Since you did so well in the shower, I think I owe you another present. How about that massage you requested when we were discussing terms for tonight?"

"Yes, please."

"Stay there." Santa leaves the table for the dresser where his bag sits. After digging in it, he pulls out a bottle of oil. He opens it as he returns to me and waves the dropper under my nose.

"You really put in the work to give the book boyfriend experience," I say after catching the scent of my favorite essential oil, ylang ylang.

"You paid. I serve."

I don't know why those simple four words turn me on so much.

Santa pours some oil into his hands and warms it in his hands by rubbing them together. Taking one foot into his hands, he massages the oil into it. His hands are firm but gentle while rubbing into the flesh of my foot. He moves up my leg, massaging my calves and thighs. Santa's fingers lightly graze the apex of my thighs until he notices me grinding into his hands.

"Not yet," he admonishes me before putting more oil in his hand and repeating everything with my other foot and leg. I breathe deeply and moan as he works my muscles over.

"You're a beautiful woman, Crissy. I'm very pleased to have met you."

I don't know what to do with his words, so I stay quiet. Santa puts both of his arms under my thick thighs, stands to his feet, then lifts me up out of the chair. He carries me to the massage table he has set up on one side of the room and lays me down on it, before leaving me for only a moment to get the massage oil. The massage resumes, starting at my hips, moving up my stomach and over my breasts.

"I love how soft you are," he says.

"Does Santa have a big girl fetish?"

"You could say that. Big girls have the warmest and gooey-est cookies."

He massages my neck, the tops of my shoulders, and my arms before having me turn over, where he spends an imaginable amount of time massaging my ass. As he moves up my back, I'm glad my rolls don't seem to bother him. The massage is sensual. Santa pulls my arms and necks back, stretching me every other which way. When he's done with my arms, he moves lower, putting the front side of my thighs and hips under his arms and lifting my bottom half up to stretch my lower back and loosen my hips.

This massage wasn't something I read in a book, but I did recently see it on social media and it left me intrigued. As Santa rotates my hips this way and that way, I understand why those women had looks of pure bliss on their faces. This is erotic, and the fact it's a stranger doing this to me only adds to that.

When Santa sets my body back down, I can feel that he's not the only one turned on by the massage. "Turn over."

I do, and I find him putting on another condom. Santa kisses me up my stomach and takes one breast into his mouth as he sinks into me. My walls are deliciously tender from the first round in the shower, adding a pleasurable pain to the ecstasy this dick-down gives me.

"Yes, Santa Daddy, just like that," I moan as he swings his hips in a circle while thrusting in and out of me. My nails dig into his back as he strokes harder.

"That's it, my little slut. Take this dick. Take. Every. Single. Inch. Of. This. Dick."

I tighten around him as I build to my next orgasm.

"There you go, baby. I feel you."

The way he talks me through it turns me on even more. "Shit," I moan.

"You're almost there. Oooh shit, you're so close."

"Fuck!"

"Cum on this dick like you like this dick."

That does it. I cum hard, shattering and free falling around him as he continues with this sweet torture of pleasure with his dick and words.

"That's a good little slut. My slut. Fuck, you make Santa Daddy so proud."

The orgasm doesn't stop. The more he strokes, the more he speaks directly in my ear like that, the longer it goes.

"Yeah baby, keep going. You're being such a good girl."

A strong shiver goes through me, the start of another orgasm while the first one is not yet finished. Liquid shoots from me down there like never before. I moan his name, alternating between *Santa Daddy* and *Idris*.

"You. Are. A. Fucking. Squirter. Too!" Santa says between strokes.

Delirium. That is the word to describe what I feel. I didn't know I could do that. It's like he's turned on something I didn't realize was off, let alone there at all. Electric tingles dance across my skin all over my body as I ride the waves of this latest orgasm. The sound of his dick splashing in the lake that's between my legs accompanies our moans.

"You got another one in you," he whispers to me. "I'm not stopping until you give me another one."

"Daddy, damn, damn, damn, damn," I pant.

"Not until you give me another one."

"I… I… oooh."

"Mm-hmm."

He keeps giving me steady strokes and droplets from between us splash up onto my stomach. I've had partners in my past, but none ever made me continuously orgasm before. I've read plenty of books with the female main characters having rolling orgasms, but I never thought it was probable. Having now experienced it myself makes me feel like the main character in my own story.

Santa keeps stroking me with his dick, building me up again. He's relentless in his pursuit of getting another orgasm out of me. This is a man who listens. Not long ago, I told him I need to be worn out when I have sex, and he's determined to do just that. "Come on. Give it to me."

This orgasm, it's right there, but is refusing to release. It's like it has a mind of its own and wants to build up even more. It's going to rip me in two, I just know it.

Santa picks up his tempo. "Little slut…"

"It's right there," I whimper.

"I want you to cum."

Oh shit. "Santa Daddy…"

"CUM," he growls.

I turn into fireworks on the Fourth of July, exploding and sparkling, orgasming so hard that I'm seeing spots. Santa fights with my shaking legs to keep inside me while he reaches his own oblivion. He collapses on me, and I nudge him to get off. We lay side-by-side, spent and panting. No words need to be said.

That was incredible.

Santa's Pleasure

Soon, the only sounds in the room are those of our snores. When I wake up the next morning, Santa is sitting on the loveseat.

"There she is."

"Mmmm." That is the only response I can manage at the moment. Looking around, I realize I'm under the covers. I don't remember doing that.

"I tucked you in. You were out."

"Thanks."

"I was tempted to wake you up this morning by having your pussy for breakfast, but I remembered you don't do well with spontaneity. Thought you seeing me coming would be best."

"Much appreciated. After last night, I don't know if I can mentally take another orgasm. What did you put in that condom?"

He chuckles. "Just Santa's magic dick."

I shake my head.

"Breakfast?" he asks.

"Yes, I'm famished."

We order room service again, eat, shower, and get dressed in contented silence. I appreciate it. My past experiences often served as a reminder that I don't like society's desire for small talk.

    We leave the room together, but as strangers. Very well satiated strangers. Not including the cost of the hotel, this was two thousand dollars well spent.

Acknowledgements

To my steamy readers, thank you for being patient with me while I worked on other stuff. Hopefully, this will give you something until my next spicy novel comes out.

Thanks to Chelsea, who hosted the writing sprints where I worked on a good portion of this book. It's always great having writer friends.

Though we have never met (he literally does not know my existence), but shoutout to R&B singer, songwriter, and producer, Tank. His *Salvage* album was on repeat as I wrote this.

This story was a fun project to do after finishing the last (hopefully final) draft of *Medusa Untold*. For a good bit of writing this, both the MCs were unnamed. I heard Idris' voice first with a line that unfortunately didn't make the cut. I may use that for the second book in this series, *Cupid's Lust*.

If you've made it this far, thank you.

Much Love.
Porsha

A Note from the Author:

Thank you for reading my book! I feel honored, truly.

Did you enjoy **Santa's Pleasure**? Be sure to leave a review on Amazon, Goodreads, Bookbub, or my Facebook Page!

You can preview and purchase the rest of my books on my website, as well as with your favorite online book retailer! Be sure to sign up for my mailing list while you are on my website. My Love Bugs get cover reveals at least a month before the public, as well as surprises and giveaways. www.porshadeun.com.

Love Lost Series
Love Lost
Love Lost Forever
Love Lost Revenge

Addict Series
Addict—A Fatal Attraction Story
Addict 2.0—Andre's Story
Addict 3.0—DeAngelo's Story
Addict 4.0—DeMario's Story

The Hot Holiday Series
Santa's Pleasure

Standalones
Intoxic
In Over Her Head

Santa's Pleasure

Children's Book
Princesses Can Do Anything!